This book belongs to

Princess Junainah Ali M.

The Royal Disney Princess Club

Every Disney Princess Treasures Her Friends

friendship

Story adaptation, crafts, and activities by Kris Hirschmann

Photography by White Light Incorporated, Bethel, CT

Design by Mark A. Neston Design

Published by Scholastic Inc., 90 Old Sherman Turnpike, Danbury, CT 06816.

For information regarding permission, write to: Disney Licensed Publishing, 114 Fifth Ave., New York, NY 10011.

ISBN-13: 978-0-545-04833-0   ISBN-10: 0-545-04833-8
U.K. ISBN-13: 978-0-545-08546-5   U.K. ISBN-10: 0-545-08546-2

Printed in Singapore

First printing, June 2008

Beauty and the Beast

A Storybook with Crafts & Activities

SCHOLASTIC INC.

New York Toronto London Auckland Sydney
Mexico City New Delhi Hong Kong Buenos Aires

Once upon a time in the French countryside, there lived a Prince who was selfish and spoiled. One night, an old beggar woman arrived at his castle. The Prince was unkind to her; so as punishment, she turned him into a terrible beast and placed a spell on the castle and all who lived there.

The old woman left behind an enchanted rose, explaining that the Prince would need to learn to love and be loved before the rose died. Otherwise, he would remain a beast forever.

As the years passed, the Prince fell into despair and lost all hope, thinking no one could ever love a beast.

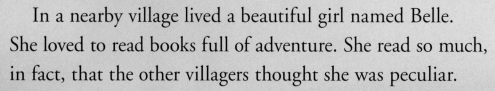

In a nearby village lived a beautiful girl named Belle.
She loved to read books full of adventure. She read so much,
in fact, that the other villagers thought she was peculiar.

"I'm not sure I fit in here," Belle confided in her father
one day. "There's no one I can really talk to."

"What about Gaston?" her father suggested.
"He's a handsome fellow."

"He's handsome, all right," Belle agreed,
". . . and conceited . . . Oh, Papa, he's
not for me!"

One snowy day, Belle's father, Maurice, set off on a journey through the woods. Before long, he was thrown from his horse and lost his way. Cold and wet, he searched for shelter. Maurice eventually came upon a gloomy-looking castle. When he hesitantly entered, he was surprised to hear, "Monsieur, you are welcome here!" He was even more surprised when he realized that his welcome had come from a candelabra!

Suddenly the Beast appeared. "*I'll* give you a place to stay," he roared and threw the old man into the dungeon.

When their horse returned home without Maurice, Belle knew something was wrong. She set out to find him and finally discovered the castle, her father, and the Beast.

"Please, let him out," begged Belle, offering herself in return for her father's freedom. So the Beast agreed.

"The castle is your home now," he growled, showing Belle to her room. Then he left her.

Feeling sad and lonely, Belle slipped out of her room later that night. She happened upon the kitchen, where she was greeted by Cogsworth the clock, Lumiere the candelabra, Mrs. Potts the teapot, and the rest of the enchanted servants. To make their guest feel welcome, they treated Belle to a dazzling show and a tasty feast.

"Bravo!" Belle said to her new friends with a smile. "That was wonderful!" Although she still missed her father very much, Belle was finding the castle to be a fascinating place.

The Beast had told Belle she was free to roam the castle—except for the West Wing. But Belle grew curious and decided to see what was in that forbidden place. Unable to resist exploring, she soon came across the enchanted rose. As she reached out to touch it, the Beast suddenly appeared. "Get out!" he roared.

Terrified, Belle fled with her horse into the snowy woods. She hadn't gone far when a pack of fierce wolves surrounded her. Just as they were about to attack, the Beast appeared out of nowhere and fought with the wolves. Though he was able to scare the pack away, the Beast was wounded during the fight.

Belle managed to get the Beast back to the castle, where she gently tended his wounds. The Beast roared in pain.

"I barely touched you!" Belle said. Then she saw the hurt in his eyes. "Thank you for saving my life," she added softly.

The Beast grunted in reply, but her words had touched his heart.

In the days that followed, the Beast began to change. With encouragement from his enchanted servants, he tried to act more like a gentleman.

One day, he surprised Belle by sharing his vast library with her.
"It's wonderful!" Belle exclaimed.

"Then it's yours," the Beast replied, happy that he had pleased her.

Finally, one evening, he found the courage to invite Belle to the
ballroom for a romantic evening of dining and dancing.

As Belle descended the staircase in a shimmering gold gown, the
Beast realized that he was beginning to fall in love with her.

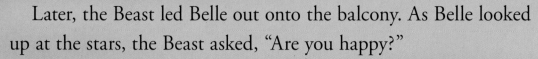

Later, the Beast led Belle out onto the balcony. As Belle looked up at the stars, the Beast asked, "Are you happy?"

"Yes," she replied, "but I wish I could see my father again."

The Beast handed Belle a magic mirror. It showed her father lying in the snow. "He's sick!" cried Belle.

"You must go to him," said the Beast, giving Belle the mirror to remember him by. Although he knew the spell would never be broken if she left, he cared for her too much to make her unhappy.

"Thank you for understanding," Belle said, and then she was gone.

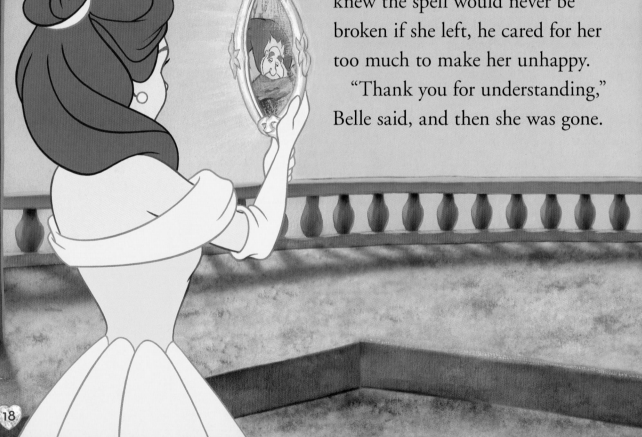

Belle soon found her father and returned home.

When Gaston heard that Belle and Maurice were back, he led an angry crowd of villagers to their door. They'd had enough of Maurice's tales of a supposed beast.

"But Papa's not crazy!" said Belle, holding up the magic mirror to show them an image of the Beast.

Everyone gasped! "We won't be safe until he's dead!" shouted Gaston.

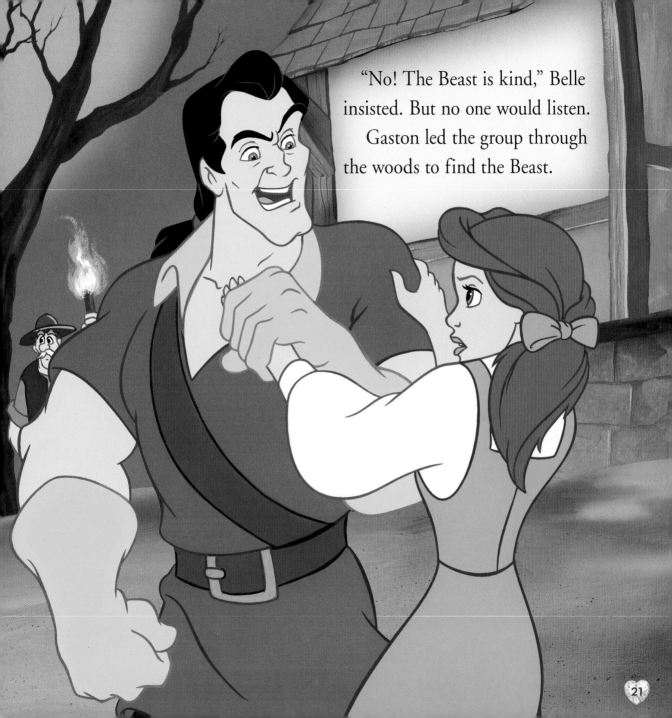

"No! The Beast is kind," Belle insisted. But no one would listen. Gaston led the group through the woods to find the Beast.

The angry mob soon stormed the castle and began battling the Beast's servants.

Gaston found the Beast in his chambers and shot him with an arrow. But the Beast was so sad about Belle that he didn't even try to defend himself.

Just then Belle appeared! Seeing her gave the Beast the strength to fight Gaston. During the fierce battle on the balcony, Gaston tumbled over the side of the castle.

The gravely wounded Beast fell to the floor. Belle ran
and knelt beside him.

"Please don't leave me! I love you!" she cried, just as the
last petal fell from the enchanted rose.

With those words, a cloud of light surrounded the Beast and he turned into a handsome prince.

"Belle! It's me!" the Prince said. He took Belle in his arms and kissed her. And as he did, the castle and the servants returned to their true forms. Love had broken the spell forever!

Later, their friends watched with delight as Belle and the Prince danced in the castle's ballroom. Belle gazed joyfully into her true love's eyes, knowing she had found the one she was meant to be with forever.

The End

Every Disney Princess Treasures Her Friends

Friendship

This month's princess theme is friendship.

These crafts and activities will show you different ways
to treasure your friends.

Belle's Crafts & Activities

Belle's friends Cogsworth, Lumiere, Mrs. Potts, and the others helped to fill her days at the castle with fun and merriment. Turn the page to discover Belle's crafts and activities all about friendship!

My Special Book

Friendship Rose

The rose is a symbol of the Beast's love for Belle. Make your own special rose to remind you how much you treasure your friends!

What You Need

- Ruler
- Scissors
- Sheet of pink or red tissue paper
- Green chenille stem (pipe cleaner)
- Green paper
- White glue

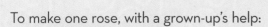

To make one rose, with a grown-up's help:

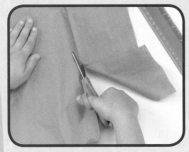

1. Measure and cut one long strip of tissue paper that is about 4 inches (10 cm) wide.

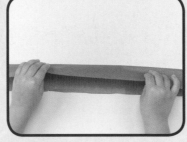

2. Fold the strip in half lengthwise.

3. Starting at one end, wrap the strip around two of your fingers. Keep wrapping until you reach the other end.

4. Pull your fingers out of the roll. Tightly wrap one end of the chenille stem (pipe cleaner) around the lower ½ inch (1.3 cm) of the roll. Bend the stem so it sticks straight down.

5. Cut two leaf shapes from the green paper. Glue the leaves to the stem.

 Royal Idea

Bend the bottom of the stem as shown in the photograph at right to make your rose stand up. Ask a grown-up to cut a clean, empty 2-liter soda bottle in half. Put the top of the bottle over your flower. You now have a magical jar for your rose, just like in the story!

The Rose Says . . .

Did you know that the color of a rose has special meaning? Make a whole bouquet of roses and give them to your friends and family members to say *Thank you, I love you,* or *You're my friend.*

- Red = Love
- Dark Pink = Thanks
- Light Pink = Happiness
- Yellow = Friendship
- White = Remembrance
- Lavender = Enchantment

My Special Book

Belle loves books. She has a few that she reads over and over again. Here's how to make a special book that you will want to read again and again.

- Four 8½- x 11-inch (22- x 28-cm) sheets of paper (any color)
- Two 8½- x 11-inch (22- x 28-cm) sheets of card stock (any color)
- Hole punch
- Three 12-inch (30-cm)-long pieces of ribbon, ⅛ inch to ¼ inch (3 mm to 6 mm) wide
- Markers, glitter, paint, stickers, and other items to decorate your book

With a grown-up's help:

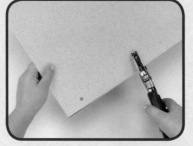

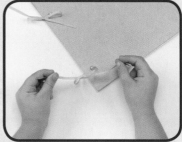

1. Hold the four sheets of paper together. Then put one sheet of card stock on top of the stack and the other card stock sheet on the bottom. (The sheets of card stock will be your book's front and back covers.)

2. Punch three holes through the entire stack as shown. (**Hint:** Use paper clips to hold the papers together while you punch the holes.)

3. Poke one piece of ribbon through each hole. Tie the ribbons loosely into bows.

4. Decorate the front cover of the book with markers, glitter, paint, stickers, or anything else you like.

5. Fill the pages of your book with things you love. You can doodle, write, glue pictures from magazines, add stickers, or do anything else you like.

Royal Idea

What would Belle love? Pretend that you are Princess Belle. You might even dress up like Belle if you would like. Then make a book all about Belle—her friends and family, stories and songs she likes, and things she loves to do. You will feel like a real princess when you work on this special project!

All About My Friends

The book on pages 32-33 is so easy to make. Why not make one for everyone you care about? Gather lots of paper, sheets of card stock, and ribbon. Put them together to make books for your friends. Decorate the books in your pals' favorite colors and styles. Then fill the books with things that are special to your friends. Give the books to your pals and wait for the smiles!

Here are some things to think about when you plan your books:

Your friend's favorite:

♡ Color
♡ Princess
♡ Place
♡ Song
♡ Movie
♡ Food

Your friend enjoys:

♡ Dressing up
♡ Arts and crafts
♡ Outdoor fun
♡ Pretend play
♡ Parties
♡ Sports
♡ Reading

Here are some ideas for a book about . . .

Your friends:
- Pictures of you and your friends together
- Drawings of things you like to do with your friends
- A list of all the things you love about your friends
- Stickers or cutout pictures showing your friends' favorite things

Your teacher:
- A drawing of your teacher
- Alphabet page—cutout letters of the alphabet placed in letter order
- Stickers that say *Good Job, A+,* and other classroom messages
- Photos of yourself at school

Your pet:
- Pictures of your pet or other animal friends
- Drawings or photos of you and your pet together
- Cutout pictures of pet toys and yummy treats
- Your pet's paw prints

Stained-Glass Sun Catcher

The Beast's castle has many stained-glass windows to catch the sunlight. Make your very own stained-glass sun catcher to decorate *your* castle.

- Scissors
- Tissue paper (any colors)
- Pencil
- White paper
- Tape
- Sheet of clear acetate (found in craft and office supply stores)
- Glue stick
- Removable tape

With a grown-up's help:

1. Cut the tissue paper into small pieces. The pieces can be any shape you like. (**Hint:** You don't need a lot of pieces. Cut just enough to cover the heart shape on page 37.)

2. Trace the heart shape on page 37 onto the white paper, then tape the clear acetate to the paper. Glue the pieces of tissue paper to the acetate, using the heart shape as a guide.

3. Cut around the edges of the finished stained-glass heart shape, leaving a tab at the top as shown. Remove the white paper.

Crafts & Activities

4. Tape the tab of the heart shape to a window. Then watch the light shine through your pretty sun catcher!

 **Royal Idea**

You can make any shape into stained glass. Just lay a piece of clear acetate over the shape. Then follow steps 1 through 3 to turn the shape into a sun catcher.

Friendship Catcher

Now that you know how to make stained glass, use your new skills to make a giant "friendship catcher" with your pals! Cut lots and lots of pieces of tissue paper. Tape the biggest piece of clear acetate you can find to a window. Then work with your friends to glue the tissue paper pieces to the acetate in any pattern you like. Every time the sun lights up your friendship catcher, you will remember the fun you had creating it with your friends.